VOICES IN
THE DARK

Voices In The dark

ISBN-13: 978-1944540951

For information about production rights, visit:
www.jzettelmaier.com

Published by Sordelet Ink
WWW.SORDELETINK.COM

Cover by David Blixt

Voices in the Dark

A Collection of Horror Radio Plays

BY

Joseph Zettelmaier

Fish Story, The Monroe County Pumpkin Queen, and Earwigs all premiered at the *Deathscribe International Festival of Horror Radio Plays*, produced by WildClaw Theatre in Chicago. **Worm Food** premiered at *Nicks and Cuts: A WildClaw Salon*, produced by WildClaw Theatre in Chicago. A Model Son, Apple Bobbers, and Bad Teeth all premiered at *The Dark Ride Radio Hour*, produced by Roustabout Theatre in Livonia, MI. The casts and designers were as follows:

FISH STORY: (2012, Winner: The Bloody Axe Award)
Directed by Kevin Theis
Original Foley Design by Ele Matelan
Foley Artists: Aly Amidei, Ele Matelan
Jim: Chris Rickett
Doc: Dave Skvarla
Cody: Joe Bianco

THE MONROE COUNTY PUMPKIN QUEEN: (2013)
Directed by Laura Hooper
Original Foley Design by Ele Matelan
Foley Artists: Sarah D. Espinoza, Allie Kunkler, Ele Matelan
Kelly: Mandy Walsh
Sue: Simone Roos
Trish: Melonie Collmann

EARWIGS: (2015, Winner: The Bloody Axe Award)
Directed by Sara Sevigny
Original Foley Design by Ele Matelan
Foley Artists: Jeffrey Gardner, Ele Matelan
Sara: Robyn Coffin
Amber: Jennifer Santanello

WORMFOOD: (2015)
Directed by Josh Zagoren
Original Foley Design by Ele Matelan
Foley Artists: Timothy C. Amos, Ele Matelan
Josiah: Kevin Alves
Lark: Krista D'Agostino
Doctor: Timothy C. Amos

A MODEL SON: (2016)
Directed by Joey Albright
Original Foley Design by Corrina Van Hamlin
Foley Artist: Corrina Van Hamlin
Tommy: Derek Ridge
Linda: Larissa Marten
Carl: Patrick Loos
Dr. Deadly: Chris Korte

APPLE BOBBERS: (2017)
Directed by Joey Albright
Original Foley Design by Corrina Van Hamlin
Foley Artists: Julia Garlotte, Corrina Van Hamlin
Becky: Meghan VanArsdalen
Jenna: Jeannine Thompson
Kim: Jaclynn Cherry
Mason: Chris Korte

BAD TEETH: (2017)
Directed by Joey Albright
Original Foley Design by Corrina Van Hamlin
Foley Artists: Julia Garlotte, Corrina Van Hamlin
Kim: Meghan VanArsdalen
Etta: Jaclynn Cherry
Dr. Billings: Jeannine Thompson
Darkness: Chris Korte

FOR INFORMATION ABOUT PRODUCTION RIGHTS,
VISIT WWW.JZETTELMAIER.COM.

FISH STORY

(A doorbell rings)

JIM
Ah, what the hell is this?

(The doorbell rings many times in succession)

JIM
Gimme a second! Christ.

DOC
Take it easy. Your hand still looks...

JIM
I know what it looks like.

(JIM opens the door. The sound of a snowstorm raging outside)

CODY
Jim! Lemme in!

JIM
Gimme a damn minute! Doc! Help me out!

DOC
What?

JIM
Goddamn snowdrift is blockin' the door!

CODY
I'm freezing my nuts off here!

JIM
Doc! Now!

DOC
All right, hold on.

(DOC & JIM force the door open. CODY enters, & they slam the door shut)

JIM
Cody?

CODY
Hey.

JIM
What're you...?

CODY
My piece of shit truck spun out. I tried to walk home, but it's the second ice age out there! You gotta let me crash here 'til it stops.

DOC
Now hold on.

CODY
I know you?

JIM
Cody, this here's Doc Mathers from over in Houghton. Doc, this is Cody.

DOC
Nice to meet you. Jim, we should probably…

CODY
What you need a doctor for? Did you…Jesus Christ, what happened to your hand?!

DOC
We really need to change those bandages.

JIM
I got bit.

CODY
By what?

JIM
Well, now…funny story there.

DOC
Jim!

JIM
It's all right. Cody's my best friend. We can trust him.

CODY
Totally. Trust me with what?

JIM
Well, Doc here…he's a veterinarian.

CODY
You don't have any pets. Not since Stumpy went tits up last year.

JIM
C'mon. Let's go to the bathroom.

(Pause)

CODY
I...I'm good, thanks.

DOC
Do you want to see this thing or not?

CODY
Just flush it and I'll take your word for it.

JIM
It's not...I caught something this morning! It's in the tub!

CODY
What?

JIM
Come on!

(They all go to the bathroom)

JIM
You ready?

CODY
I guess?

(They move the shower curtain. Splashing in the tub)

CODY
Would you look at that...

JIM
Pretty damn impressive. Am I right?

CODY
What the hell is it?

JIM
I don't know! That's why I called Doc here. We been trying to figure it out all day.

DOC
I'll be honest, I've never seen anything like it.

CODY
It's a fish. I mean, ugliest damn fish I ever seen, but...

DOC
Yes, but whatever kind of fish it is, it's unique. At least
to these waters.

JIM
I was out on the lake this morning, and...

(More splashing)

JIM
Settle down, ugly. Been doin' that all day. That's why
we put that glass window on top of the tub. Otherwise,
the stupid thing would've flopped on the ground and...
Anyway, so I'm on the lake, sittin' in my shack and I'm
coming up empty. Just when I'm about to pack it up...
BAM! Something grabs my line. I mean, I damn near
lost my pole! This thing pulls like a mother! So I fight
with it for, I shit you not, an hour and...well, when I
pulled up that ugly cuss there, my jaw hit the ground.
I tried to get the hook out and it damn near took off
my hand.

CODY
Wait...that's what bit you?

DOC
Whatever this thing is, it's aggressive. You should see
what it does when you turn off the lights.

CODY
I don't follow.

DOC
For some reason, it gets more docile when the lights are on. When we left it in the dark, it almost broke through that window. I think it must be some sort of bottom-dweller. It's not used to anything brighter than a flash-light.

CODY
What're those? Those little holes along its belly.

DOC
I have no idea. We've had some trouble getting it still long enough to examine. At first I thought it was some sort of freshwater angler fish, with its spherical body and...well, those huge teeth. But anglers are salt-water fish and not usually this massive.

JIM
It's like a big, scaly ball of mean.

DOC
What I think we have here is either a new species...or a very old one.

CODY
For real?

DOC
Back in the 70s, they found a fish in Asia...one that was supposed to be extinct for millions of years. I think we might have a similar situation here.

JIM
I'm gettin' a beer. Who wants one?

CODY
Sure.

DOC
I'm fine.

CODY
Something like this worth money?

(Pause)

DOC
Why do you ask?

CODY
I bet like a college or something would pay good money for a dinosaur fish.

DOC
Um, yes, possibly. But just so we're clear, Jim discovered it. And I examined it.

CODY
So?

DOC
So any money is split fifty-fifty. Me and Jim.

(Beat)

CODY
You tryin' to cut me out?

DOC
Cut you out of what? You didn't do anything!

CODY
I was here at the time of the…idea-making.

DOC
No you weren't! Jim and I decided this before you even showed up.

CODY
You remind me of my dad. Changed his will at the last second and my bitch stepmom got all my money. Well, Cody Stubbs won't get screwed again!

DOC
Just calm down now, son. Look at this realistically. You didn't...

CODY
Jim! We gotta talk! Jim!

(They go back to the living room)

CODY
Jesus Christ! Jim?

DOC
Get him up on the couch.

(JIM moans as they move him)

DOC
He's burning up. Let's get those bandages off.

(A wet sound as the bandages pull away. They react to the awful smell)

CODY
Oh Christ. I'm gonna be sick.

DOC
Look at his arm!

CODY
No way. No goddamn way.

DOC
That's necrosis is what that is. It's rotting off.

JIM
...I don't...feel right...

CODY
Jim! You're gonna be ok! Just...

(JIM vomits)

CODY
That's it, buddy. Let it out.

DOC
We have to get him to a hospital.

(He checks the phone)

DOC
Storm's knocked out the phones! And I can't get a signal for my cell!

CODY
'Course not, all the way out here. *(To JIM)* Hang in there, buddy.

JIM
What'd...that damn fish...do to me?

CODY
What?

DOC
The infection...it's starting from where the fish bit him.

CODY
So...it's a poisonous dinosaur fish?

DOC
Maybe? I don't know!

CODY
Jim buddy, if you don't make it, can I have your half of

the fish money?

JIM
…gimme some…water…

CODY
You heard him! He said yes!

(A loud crash outside)

DOC
What the hell was that?

CODY
Storm took down an old tree and…

(The house loses power)

DOC
No. No no no no no.

CODY
Relax. Jim's got a generator outside. I fixed it for him a bunch.

DOC
Outside? There's four feet of snow outside!

CODY
Well, it's that or freeze to death!

(A loud crash from the bathroom)

CODY
What the hell was that?

DOC
I don't know. I can't see anything.

CODY
Sounded like it came from the bathroom. *(Pause)* You said that fish got real mean in the dark, right?

(A strange scuttling sound)

CODY
Jesus Christ! You hear that?

DOC
I heard something. What was it?

(More scuttling)

CODY
Shit! It's in the room!

DOC
Is there...gimme a flashlight!

CODY
Hold on. Jim keeps one on his...

(CODY crashes into something)

CODY
Dammit! It's around here somewhere.

DOC
Hurry up!

CODY
Keep your shirt on! I'm tryin' to...

(A crunching, chewing sound. JIM moans weakly)

CODY
Oh man. Oh man.

DOC
Get the damn flashlight!

(CODY searches in the dark)

CODY
Found it! Come on, you piece of...

(CODY hits the light. It turns on. They scream)

CODY
Oh god! JIM!

DOC
How did that fish get out here!?

CODY
It's eating Jim!

(The fish hisses, then more scuttling sounds)

CODY
Holy shit! Did you see that! It's got legs! Like spider legs or...

DOC
Those holes on its underside....It can pull its legs into itself.

CODY
What the hell kind of fish is this?!

DOC
Keep your light on it! It doesn't like the light!

(The sound of the fish scuttling and breathing deeply)

CODY
It's breathing, isn't it? It's breathing air!

DOC
Keep your light on it!

CODY
I don't know where it is!

DOC
Jim? You hang in there! Give me some light!

CODY
How's he doing?

DOC
Oh god....Jim, I...

CODY
Christ almighty...It tore his whole damn throat out.

DOC
We have to get out of here!

CODY
And go where? Ain't another house for ten miles! We'll
freeze before...

DOC
What? What is it?

CODY
My truck! It can't move, but it's got a full tank of gas.
The heater works fine. It'll get us through til...

(More scuttlng)

DOC
It's moving again.

CODY
Where?!

DOC
I don't know! Hold your light still! *(Pause)* It's over
there!

CODY
Where?

DOC
I think it went behind the couch! Check!

CODY
I don't see it.

(DOC clubs CODY with a beer bottle)

CODY
AH! Dammit! What the hell are you doin'?

(DOC hits him again)

CODY
Stop!

DOC
Just lie down, you dumb hick!

(They struggle)

DOC
Once it starts...eating you...I can get out...

CODY
Son of a bitch!

(DOC slams him into a wall)

DOC
Come on! Come on! Lights out!

(CODY hits DOC with the flashlight)

DOC
Ah! Dammit! What are you...?

(CODY hits him again)

CODY
Mag-lites hit pretty good! Didn't even bust the bulb. C'mon, fishy!

(CODY hits him again)

CODY
Dinner's ready!

(One more hit. DOC drops)

CODY
There ya go, you ugly bastard. Eat up.

(More scuttling and crunching as the fish starts to eat DOC)

CODY
Yep. Just keep on stuffin' your face while I think this through. Just gotta...

(Very loud eating noises)

CODY
Oh man. Just...ok. Jim and Doc are dead, which means I get to keep all the money for this thing. But I can't get near it without gettin' bit. And if I get bit, I'm gonna go all rotten like Jim. Shit! There's gotta be some way I can...*(Pause)* Know what? I bet a college will still pay for a dead fish-monster.

(CODY hits the fish. It hisses)

CODY
Hey! Stop! Just...come on, you ugly...

(CODY yells, then hits it very hard. It drops)

CODY
Holy shit! I did it! HA! I did it!

(He hits it a few more times)

CODY
That's the fuckin' end of fuckin' that! Try to bite me? How you like that Maglite to the face, ugly? Huh?

(CODY laughs, then collects himself)

CODY
Ah, Jim. I'm sorry as hell that you got killed. But I didn't do it. The fish did it. Killed you and the Doc. I can tell the cops that with a clear conscience. And then I killed the fish, so... I don't know. If it makes ya feel better, that dead thing is gonna make me a big ol' pile of money. Just gonna find a sled or something and drag it back to my truck. You keep sleds in your garage, I bet. Lemme just...

(CODY pushes on the door but can't get it open)

CODY
Open... you... rat bastard! Damn! Goddamn snow's blocking the door! *(Beat)* All right, Cody. Keep it together. Gotta be another way out of here. Maybe I can bust out a window. What do you think, you dumb, ugly dead thing? Wanna take a trip out...

(The scuttling sound returns)

CODY
What the hell...?

(CODY shines the light on the spot where the fish was but it's gone)

CODY
No. No no no no no. You were dead, fishy. You weren't breathing or...

(More scuttling)

CODY
Fuck me! Where the hell are you?! How can something as big as you just up and disa...?!

(The scuttling stops. Heavy breathing behind CODY)

CODY
You're right behind me, ain't ya?

(The creature hisses)

CODY
Dammit. Screwed again.

(CODY screams as the fish attacks him. A struggle, then CODY goes silent. The sound of the fish breathing and starting to eat)

THE END

THE
MONROE COUNTY
PUMPKIN QUEEN

(Music playing on a radio. KELLY is waking up slowly)

KELLY
Oh god...what...

(SUE is whistling to the music)

KELLY
...where am I...What...?

SUE
Oh! You're awake.

KELLY
...I was asleep?

SUE
Don't feel bad. That much chloroform would knock out a...person...like a person who...never mind.

(KELLY struggles. She's tied to a chair)

SUE
You're tied to a chair.

KELLY
What?!

SUE
Here. Let me get the light.

(She turns on a light)

KELLY
What the hell is this?

SUE
Well, I like to think of it as a multi-purpose barn-green-house-lab, but...

KELLY
What the hell am I...Wait. I know you.You teach math at the high school.

SUE
Science. I teach science.

KELLY
You kidnapped me!

SUE
I sure did.

KELLY
Why? Know what? Doesn't matter. My husband is rich. Very rich.You don't have to say a word to me. He'll be able to...

SUE
OK. I feel like I should just say, right off, that this isn't a ransom situation. I don't want you to get your hopes up.

(The sound of liquids boiling)

SUE
Oops. Let me just get that.

KELLY
Why...why shouldn't I get my hopes up?

SUE
Ow. Ow ow ow. Hot. Very hot.

KELLY
What are you going to do to me?

SUE
Could you just...I need a minute. This is very delicate work.

(She mixes chemicals)

KELLY
What the fuck is this?!

SUE
Oh my god. The mouth on you.

KELLY
Let me go right fucking now!

SUE
What part of "delicate work" don't you understand!? Believe me, you want me to get the dosage right.

KELLY
HELP! Somebody help me!

SUE
Listen. I didn't gag you because that seemed rude. I'm willing to revisit the idea.

(KELLY quiets down. SUE turns off the music)

SUE
Sorry, I'm really into oldies. I know it's not everyone's cup of tea, but it's really useful for the growing process.

KELLY
What are you growing?

SUE
All sorts of things. Botany is my specialty, not that you care.

KELLY
I care. I absolutely care. I have a Japanese Oak in my front yard that...

SUE
Don't bond with me, ok? It won't change what's going to happen.

KELLY
Um...what is going to happen?

(Pause)

SUE
You know what your problem is? You've got pretty girl syndrome. You're too used to getting your way. How many years, Kelly? How many years have you been the Monroe County Pumpkin Queen?

(Beat)

KELLY
I...what?

SUE
Seven. Seven years in a row, sweeping away the competition with these giant pumpkins that aren't even yours!

KELLY
That's not true! I...

SUE
Please. You couldn't grow moss if I left your corpse on

the north side of a tree.

KELLY
What?!

SUE
Do you know what it's like coming in second, third, fourth to you and your socialite buddies? None of you care about agriculture. You just need to shove one more crown on your fat, coiffed heads.

KELLY
I tell you what. Next year, I won't even compete. I'll tell my friends to drop out too. You'll be a shoe-in!

SUE
You really don't need to worry about next year.

(KELLY starts to cry)

SUE
Stop it.

KELLY
I've never done anything to you! Just let me go! Please!

SUE
You never...?! Are you serious? Are you flippin' serious?!

KELLY
I don't even know your name!

SUE
It's Sue! Sue Murtaugh! I've been teaching science at Monroe High for nine years! And you...!

(The liquids boil again)

SUE
Darn it! Stop distracting me.

KELLY
Sue...can I call you Sue?

SUE
No.

KELLY
Whatever there is between us, we can talk it through. I actually volunteer down at the VA hospital and...

SUE
God, I want to shove a civic trophy down your throat.

(A timer goes off)

SUE
Finally! You have no idea how complicated it is, making this stuff.

KELLY
What are you making?

(Pause)

SUE
Are you asking because you're really interested, or are you just trying to engage me so I don't...?

KELLY
Really interested. Really just...yes, super interested.

SUE
Because I'm not going to lie, I'd love to talk about this. Do you mind? I mean, you're not going anywhere.

KELLY
We can talk about anything. Anything at all.

SUE
It's just...Kelly, I never wanted to be a science teacher. I just did it to pay the bills, but real science...that's my

love. I wrote this incredible thesis about...do you know what kleptoplasty is?

KELLY
Is...is it the thing where you have to steal all the time?

SUE
No. It's a rare process in which certain animals, sea slugs for example, absorb plant matter rather than just ingesting it. What happens then...it's so fascinating... they essentially become part animal, part plant. They can actually use photosynthesis. Can you believe it?! A freaking animal using photosynthesis!

KELLY
That's...wow. Awesome.

SUE
I know! So here I am, promising grad student at the time, and I start to wonder where does animal end and plant begin? And can we blur that line? Can we maybe even flip it completely?

KELLY
Can....can you?

(TRISH moans in the corner)

KELLY
The hell was that?

SUE
Ignore it. Not important. Now, you were asking if I...

TRISH
...been waiting...so long...

SUE
...could blur the line between..

TRISH
...Get where I'm going...

KELLY
What the hell is that?!

SUE
I said leave it alone! I'm trying to...

TRISH
Sunshine...LOVE!

SUE
Trish! Shut up already!

KELLY
Who's Trish?

SUE
(Sighs) Ok. Fine. So last year, there was this punk kid selling weed behind the school's organic garden. MY organic garden. Trish Heydenfeld. Dropped out of high school five years ago, but she...

(TRISH tries to sing the Sunshine of Your Love guitar solo)

TRISH
Duh duh duh duh duh duh duh duh duh duh...

KELLY
She's....Is that her? Under that blanket?

TRISH
Sunshine....love!

SUE
Sort of?

KELLY
Oh god oh god oh god...

SUE
I just...I covered her up because I didn't want to freak you out. More, I mean.

KELLY
You're kidnapping women! And torturing them! Us!

SUE
No. Absolutely not. I'm not that kind of person. But sometimes sacrifices have to be made so science can move forward.

KELLY
Trish?! Can you hear me?

SUE
Don't talk to it.

KELLY
We've got to work together so...

TRISH
Duh duh duh duh duh duh duh duh duh duh...

SUE
Yeah, she's not gonna be much help.

KELLY
What did you do to her?

SUE
I took a wasted life, and tried to make something good out of it.

KELLY
Show me.

SUE
You don't want that. Really.

KELLY
Show me!

(Pause)

SUE
Fine.

(SUE removes the tarp covering TRISH)

KELLY
Oh my god!

SUE
I told you you wouldn't...

KELLY
What is that?!

SUE
Kelly, meet Trish.

KELLY
That's not...Jesus Christ! That's not a person.

TRISH
...getting near dark...

SUE
Really? What do you think it is?

KELLY
Like...some kind of...huge rotten tree...with a face...?

SUE
Actually, she was supposed to be a two hundred pound pumpkin.

TRISH
...light close her tired eyes...

KELLY
Hold on...one of her feeding tubes popped out...

(SUE pokes the tube into TRISH, who moans or cries out)

SUE
This, Kelly. This is real science.

KELLY
You did this to her?

SUE
Not my finest work. I mean, she's definitely becoming some sort of gourd, but look at those tumors. And those oozing sores. She's bigger than I'd expected, but she's pretty hideous.

TRISH
...hurts....food hurts...

SUE
I know, sweetie. This is why I couldn't enter the contest this year. No way was my pumpkin ready.

KELLY
You're turning her into a...!? Oh god...I...I'm gonna...

(KELLY vomits)

SUE
I know. The smell takes some getting used to. But the good news is, I figured out what was wrong with the process. I rushed it. Took six months for Trish to... become what she's becoming. But I've got a whole year with you.

(Pause)

KELLY
What?

SUE
I'll be feeding you the serum in slower, steadier doses. It will take longer, but the results will be worth it.

KELLY
You can't be serious.

SUE
Sure I can.

KELLY
Please! Please! For fuck's sake, I…

(SUE gags KELLY)

SUE
You've got to stop swearing. You're upsetting Trish.

TRISH
…feel bad…hurt all over…

SUE
This is actually the chattiest she's been in a while. She used to talk all the time. She'd try to explain what was happening…really useful for my notes. And she'd swear a lot. Like you. But when the metamorphosis got more aggressive…now she mostly just sings. Honestly, that's pretty impressive considering most of her nervous system is plant fiber now.

TRISH
Mommy…feel sick…

SUE
I know. She's been bloating lately. I think that's why she smells so bad. Gaseous buildup in her pulp. But I've already corrected for that so…

TRISH
Hurts! Hurts all over!

SUE
Wow, you really upset her. Trish honey, can you… Trish, look at me.

(TRISH moans in pain. SUE snaps her fingers, getting TRISH's attention)

SUE
Can you describe what's happening to you?

TRISH
I've been…

SUE
What?

TRISH
…waiting so long…

SUE
No! No Sunshine of Your Love! What's happening to you right now?

TRISH
Trish hurts…insides hurt…

SUE
OK, you've got to calm down. The more you shake, the more those sores open up.

TRISH
AH! HURTS! HURTS SO BAD!

SUE
Just take a deep breath and…

TRISH
MOMMY! MOMMY, I…

(The sound of a massive pumpkin exploding, sending innards everywhere. KELLY cries out, still gagged)

SUE
Well poop. I really hoped that wouldn't happen. Here, let me clean you up.

(KELLY manages to get the gag off)

KELLY
Jesus fucking Christ! She exploded!

SUE
Don't worry. That won't happen to you.

KELLY
Please! I'll do anything! Anything you want! Just...

SUE
God, this place is going to stink for a month.

KELLY
Are you listening?! I have money! Lots of money! I'll do anything!

SUE
Kelly, you've done so much already. Like casting the deciding vote that cancelled my science club.

KELLY
I...what?

SUE
Why they let an ignoramus like you on the school board, I'll never know. But you just get whatever you want, don't you, you social climbing little...

KELLY
I'll fix it! Let me just...!

SUE
This is why I decided you should be the next test subject. You committed the worst sin of all you actively contrib-

uted to the growth of ignorance. "Oh no! We didn't score high enough on the standardized tests! Better cut the non-essentials!" That's what you called my program, Kelly. That's what you called me. Non. Essential.

KELLY
I didn't mean to...The city is broke! We had to make cuts somewhere!

SUE
It's funny hearing a woman who drives a Mercedes say the word "broke."

KELLY
It's not too late! I can run some numbers!

SUE
Winning the Pumpkin Queen Crown every single year...I could've gotten past that. Maybe. But when you shut down my program...

(The sound of water misters spraying)

KELLY
What the hell...?

SUE
Those are the ceiling misters. They're on a timer. Trust me, once the transformation takes hold, you'll be glad for the water.

KELLY
My husband's going to find me. Or the police.

SUE
Just like they found Trish?

(Beat)

SUE
You've…you've actually got a little Trish in your hair.
Let me get that.

KELLY
They will! My Nathan won't stop looking until…

SUE
This place is almost impossible to find. And to be honest,
even if they do find it…well, before too long, you're not
going to be all that identifiable.

KELLY
No. No no no no…

SUE
The limbs atrophy first, then just kind of…slough off.
So no fingerprints. And DNA? Yeah, that changes even
faster. The person they'll be looking for? You won't be
her anymore. Or ever again.

(The timer dings again)

SUE
OK. I just have to mix the individual parts and we'll get
started.

(During the following, SUE mixes chemicals)

KELLY
I'm going to kill you.

SUE
Mm-hmm.

KELLY
Listen to me. I'm going to get out of this, and I'm going
to murder you.

SUE
If you say so.

KELLY
I'm going to fucking murder you, you bitch!

(SUE gags KELLY roughly)

SUE
I want to be honest with you, Kelly. This is going to be very, very painful. And it's not really going to get any easier. Over the course of the next year, your genes will be irrevocably altered, and it's going to hurt. Your bones will slowly dissolve, your organs will burst as they make room for vegetable fibers, and most of your epidermis will slide off as your new "skin" grows beneath it. I don't know if this will be any comfort, but you're going to lose your mind as well. I watched it happen to Trish. When the serum starts to mutate your nervous system…your sense of self is going to start to disappear. Memories will fade, along with whatever shred of intellect you have. It's not pretty. But I want you to remember this for as long as you can.

(SUE turns on the music, playing softly)

SUE
I'm going to be right here. I'll take care of you, keep you watered, give you light and music and…in a weird way, this process is going to make us very close. Now if needles freak you out, go ahead and close your eyes.

(She sticks an IV into KELLY, who cries out)

SUE
Sorry. I know that stings. In about a minute, you're going to feel the serum in your bloodstream. It's going to begin the change, and I just…Kelly, thank you for

letting me talk. I haven't had anyone to talk to since the pain drove Trish nuts. It's been nice. Really nice.

(KELLY begins to convulse)

SUE
OK. There it goes. Don't fight it. Just let it happen.

(KELLY moans in pain)

SUE
I know this is really difficult, but look on the bright side. Next year, we're going to win Pumpkin Queen of Monroe County together. Won't that be nice?

(KELLY screams in agony)

SUE
It'll be really nice.

THE END

EARWIGS

SARA

(Narrating) If there was one sentence…one grouping of words…a moment that doomed us, it was this.

AMBER

This place is perfect.

SARA

(Narrating) Amber loved the house as soon as she saw it. Not a house…a cottage. Our dream. A little place in the woods. And Amber loved it.

AMBER

Absolutely perfect.

SARA

(Narrating) But the minute I set foot inside…I don't know. I could see the beauty of the place. And the smell of the forest, the hardwood…everything. On the surface, it was like out of a painting. But under the surface…

(The sound of boards creaking)

AMBER
Listen to those floorboards!

(More creaking)

AMBER
It's so...rustic!

SARA
It really is.

AMBER
We did it. We really did it.

SARA
Mmm-hmm.

AMBER
What? What is it?

SARA
Does something feel...off?

AMBER
...no?

SARA
Never mind. It's great. Really.

AMBER
Yes it is. Yes. It. is. Listen to that.

(Window opens. The sound of birds outside)

AMBER
That is the sound of not worrying about crap. The birds
are saying, "Sara, no more traffic jams and smog and..."

SARA
You speak bird?

AMBER
Fluently. They say Dr. Ambrose was right.

SARA
Mmm-hmm.

AMBER
They say big city living can exacerbate pre-existing anxiety disorders.

SARA
"Exacerbate?" Those are some smart birds.

AMBER
It's not an exact translation.

SARA
Ah.

(They kiss)

AMBER
This place will help. I know it.

SARA
OK.

AMBER
And if you hate it, we can always...

SARA
Thank you.

AMBER
I'm just saying...

SARA
Amber. Thank you.

(They kiss again)

SARA
Gimme the grand tour already.

AMBER
Of the cottage, or...?

SARA
Come on.

AMBER
OK. Let's start at the basement and work our way up.

SARA
Why?

AMBER
Bedroom's upstairs. Duh.

SARA
Ok...I think this one leads to the basement...

(A creaky door opens. The sound of small things falling out of the door frame)

SARA
What the hell...OH MY GOD!

(They scream)

AMBER
OK. They're just earwigs.

SARA
God! Get them off me!

AMBER
Don't panic. They're harmless.

SARA
GET THEM OFF!

(They swat the bugs off her clothes)

AMBER
OK. They're gone. You're OK.

SARA
Are you sure!? There were like a million of them and...

AMBER
Hand to god. All gone.

SARA
I need to just...give me a minute...

(She breathes deeply, collecting herself)

AMBER
I know they're creepy as shit, but they're harmless. Honestly.

SARA
I heard that they...

AMBER
They don't crawl into your ears and lay eggs in your brain.

SARA
...crawl into your...that's what I heard!

AMBER
Totally not true. They just burrow in wood. They eat other bugs. They're one hundred percent harmless. OK?

SARA
Yeah...yeah, ok.

AMBER
You were just startled. That's all.

SARA
I know. Because I really did hear that they...

AMBER
They don't. They don't actually go anywhere near your ears. Our brains are safe from egg-laying, ok?

SARA
Ok.

AMBER
First thing tomorrow, I'll call the exterminator.

SARA
To kill them with fire?

AMBER
Yes, baby. To kill them with fire.

SARA
(Narrating) I...struggle with anxiety problems. I've tried every pill, every therapy, but...Amber was the first person I ever met who kept me calm. She has this way about her that just...I would look at her, and everything else wasn't there. Just her. Buying the cottage...we both always wanted to live in the woods, away from it all, but Amber made it happen. For me.

(Pause. The sounds of nature)

SARA
(Narrating) That night, after checking every inch of the cottage and...maybe a couple Xanex...Amber and I turned in for the night. She left the windows open, thought the sounds of the great outdoors would be soothing. Dammit, she was right. There's this river nearby and...it was amazing. I was asleep in minutes. That kind of sleep where everything just disappears. Darkness, and peace, and...

(A strange chewing sound)

SARA
(Narrating) That. That sound. Masticating. Gnashing. I don't know. It's hard to describe, but it was strange enough that it woke me right up. I could hear it in the room somewhere, but...

(Pause)

SARA
(Narrating) People often mistake fear for anxiety. They're not the same thing...similar, yes, but not the same. The big difference? Fear is a response to a very real, definite threat. Anxiety is this apprehension, a panic created by something you cannot see, cannot identify...but you know it's there all the same.

(Pause)

SARA
(Narrating) You know it, even if no one else does.

(Pause)

SARA
(Narrating) So I reached over...turned on the light...

(Click of a light switch)

SARA
(Narrating) And I saw it. I don't care what anyone else says. I saw it! This thing...this little fucking insect... crawling into Amber's ear. Not just crawling...chewing. Working its way into her...

(SARA screams. AMBER wakes up)

AMBER
Baby?! What...?!

SARA
Get it out! It's inside your...!

AMBER
What happened?! Talk to me!

SARA
There's something inside your ear!

AMBER
What?!

SARA
An earwig! I saw it crawling up your ear and...!

AMBER
Oh christ...Sara...you had a nightmare. That's all.

SARA
No! I saw it! It's...

(The sound of struggling on the bed)

AMBER
Hey! Get off me!

SARA
We have to get it out!

AMBER
Sara!

SARA
It's going to lay eggs in your brain!

AMBER
SARA!

SARA
Let me go!

AMBER
You have to calm down, baby. Look at my ear.

SARA
I don't see anything.

AMBER
Exactly. Because there's nothing in there. Because earwigs don't...

SARA
I saw it!

AMBER
It was a panic attack or a night terror or something. But there's nothing inside me, ok? The whole earwig thing...it's a myth. That's all.

SARA
(Narrating) But that wasn't all. I knew it in my heart. Yes, I get it. Rationally, it didn't hold up. But I knew what I saw. Eventually, Amber went back to sleep. Me? I lied there, staring at the ceiling, counting my breaths, but I never went under. I just...I kept replaying that horrible sound in my head.

(The odd chewing sound returns)

SARA
(Narrating) That sound. The next morning, I went to work while Amber got to it, fixing up the cottage. When I got back...

AMBER
Did I what?

SARA
Did you call the exterminator?

AMBER
Oh. Yeah. No, I figured I could handle it myself.

SARA
Amber...

AMBER
They're harmless! Creepy, sure, but they don't do, like, anything. I'll get some Raid or a bug bomb and....

SARA
Those things are infesting this cottage!

AMBER
Ok, "infesting" is maybe a little strong. We saw them in one door.

SARA
What about last night?

AMBER
You had a night terror. That's all.

SARA
(Narrating) There was something about her tone...she was telling me to drop it. And I did. I shouldn't have, but...you know how it is. You love someone, and when they give you a clear signal not to push, you don't. That was my mistake.

(Pause)

SARA
(Narrating) Things got worse over the next few weeks. I kept hearing things. Not the chewing, but...

(The sound of many insects scuttling)

SARA
(Narrating) They were everywhere. In the walls, in the

floors. Amber assured me there was nothing wrong; she even pulled up the boards to show me. Every time, there was nothing there, but...

(More scuttling)

SARA
(Narrating) I could hear it! I wasn't imagining it! They were there, and Amber was covering up for them! I know how that sounds, but you weren't there. You didn't see how she changed. She never got any bug spray or anything. Made no attempt to kill these things. And she stopped...she could see that I was freaking out, and she just didn't care.

AMBER
Let it drop, Sara.

SARA
(Narrating) That was her go-to response to my fears.

AMBER
Just let it drop.

SARA
(Narrating) There was this distance growing between us. I thought...at first, I thought it was because...I blamed myself. I thought she couldn't handle me anymore. But that wasn't it. Amber was the most patient, caring human being you'd ever meet. Mother Teresa was a cold-hearted beast by comparison. So I started spying on her. Amber, not Mother Teresa. I'd act like I was going to bed, but I'd just peak around the banister and watch her. Watch her talking to...something.

(Strange clicking noises)

SARA
(Narrating) That's what she sounded like. She'd kneel down, facing the basement, and just...

(Strange clicking noises)

SARA
(Narrating) Please believe me; this was no nightmare. This was the woman I loved acting like she was possessed. Not just the distance. My therapist said that's not uncommon when a couple moves in together, for there to be some shortness while we adjusted to each other. He said the worst thing I could do was fixate, to obsess on these little differences. But they weren't little! This wasn't a realization that Amber was different than I thought... she was changing. Something was changing her.

(Nature sounds. SARA climbs in bed)

SARA
Amber. Amber!

AMBER
What?

SARA
We need to talk.

AMBER
No.

SARA
I'm serious.

AMBER
You're always serious. It's killing me. Go back to sleep.

SARA
Something's wrong.

AMBER
No.

SARA
With you. Something's wrong with you.

AMBER
No. Go to sleep.

SARA
I saw you.

AMBER
Saw me what?

SARA
I saw you eating.

AMBER
Shocking.

SARA
Spiders. I saw you eating spiders.

AMBER
You're being nuts.

SARA
Don't. Don't call me that.

AMBER
I don't want to fight. I want to sleep.

SARA
I saw you picking spiders out of their webs in the living room. I saw you toss them right into your mouth.

AMBER
It's your new meds. They're fucking you up.

SARA
Stop dismissing this! You ate fucking spiders, Amber! This is a big deal.

AMBER
I'll call Dr. Ambrose tomorrow. He'll...

SARA
NO! I'm not...stop it! I'm not insane!

(Pause)

AMBER
You might be.

SARA
...What?

AMBER
These last few weeks...I see you. I see you watching me when you think I'm not paying attention. And every day is a new litany of things you're freaking out about, or things I'm doing, or...I don't think you can hear yourself, and I'm worried.

SARA
You're worried?! Try being with someone who's eating bugs!

AMBER
I'M NOT EATING BUGS! I'm not doing anything but...

(Pause)

AMBER
We're falling apart.

SARA
No. It's something else. Something that...

AMBER
This isn't some outside influence, Sara. We...you and I...
we're not working.

SARA
Don't say that.

AMBER
It's true. You know it's true.

SARA
No! It's you! It's something inside of you, changing you!

AMBER
Like what?

(Pause)

AMBER
I'm dying to know, Sara. What do you think is changing me?

(Pause)

SARA
I think they're inside you.

AMBER
What?! What's inside me?!

SARA
Earwigs.

AMBER
...jesus fucking christ...

SARA
That night, I saw one go into your ear! I think it laid
eggs...

AMBER
Stop.

SARA
...inside your brain! I think that's why your personality is changing!

AMBER
Sara, stop.

SARA
These eggs are like growing or eating parts of your brain and...

AMBER
No! That's just...Is it really easier for you to believe that some urban legend is burrowing in my head than to accept the fact that you need help?! Real, serious help.

SARA
I'm not crazy!

AMBER
And I'm not the host mother for a colony of insects!

(Pause)

AMBER
I'm leaving.

SARA
...what?

AMBER
I already talked with my mom. I can move back home for a bit and...

SARA
You can't! This is our place! This is our life together!

AMBER
I just can't...I can't be there for you anymore. It's too much. I'm sorry, I'm not strong enough.

SARA
This isn't you talking.

AMBER
It is, Sara. And I need you to hear me. There's nothing wrong with needing help...

SARA
Don't.

AMBER
But you need more than I can give you.

SARA
Don't do this to me.

AMBER
I'll call you tomorrow, ok? When I get to my mom's. We can...

SARA
Don't! Don't leave me!

(Pause)

SARA
(Narrating) And then it happened.

AMBER
This isn't the end. We just...

(AMBER starts to gag)

SARA
Amber?

AMBER
I just...I'm worked up and...

(AMBER gags harder)

SARA
Baby? BABY?!

(AMBER screams. The sound of AMBER thrashing & convulsing)

SARA
(Narrating) I thought she was having a seizure or something. Her eyes went bone white and she just writhed on the ground, grabbing at her head. I ran for the phone, called 911. They said they were on their way. I turned back to her and she screamed...

AMBER
Sara! SARA!

SARA
(Narrating) That was the last thing she ever said.

(AMBER's screams are cut short)

SARA
(Narrating) I saw her eyes clear, she looked right at me, and...I saw them. Hundreds, thousands, I don't know. But they were inside her, trying to get out, burrowing their way out and...

(AMBER's head explodes. The sound of a multitude of insects falling to the ground)

SARA
(Narrating, fighting back tears) She exploded. She just... her whole head erupted into this swarm of...I'd been right. The whole time, I was right. Those things had been inside her the whole time, gestating, growing, and...

(Pause)

SARA

When the paramedics arrived, they saw me sitting there, sobbing, covered in Amber's blood. Her body was just lying there, her face this wreck and…I tried to tell them. I tried to make them understand, but the fucking earwigs had already scattered. Into the floor, into the shadows.

(Pause)

SARA

I'm here for psychiatric evaluation, until the trial. None of it makes any sense to them, not that it makes much sense to me. There are things that have to be seen to be believed, I suppose. But that won't be a problem.

(The strange chewing sound)

SARA

(Narrating) See, earwigs are really tiny. I didn't even notice the one that had crawled into my hair when Amber died. Rode with me all the way to the hospital, to the jail, and…it's in here now. Inside my head. I can feel it…not a dull, unspecified dread, but a very real fear. And in a few days…maybe less…everyone will know that I was right.

(The chewing grows louder)

SARA
(Narrating) I was right all along.

(The chewing grows louder still)

THE END

WORM FOOD

(Civil War style music plays)

JOSIAH *(Reading)*
From the journal of Lt. Josiah T. Walker, 10th Mississippi Infantry. I have waited a long time to put down the events of April 7th, 1862. Perhaps too long. I have always known that any who would read this will likely think me a madman. To them, I say this: I am not mad, and it is my dearest hope that in revealing this story, I may free myself of it. Please know that I will not embellish or misrepresent what has happened to me. These words I write are the truth, though I wish to God Almighty that they were not.

(Gunfire sounds under the music)

JOSIAH *(Reading)*
The battle for Shiloh was lost. With the arrival of General Grant's army, and the great losses on the Confederate side, we knew the day was done. My own dear brother fell to a Yankee bayonet. I do not know if that was the

catalyst, but something within me broke that bloody day. Colonel Smith sounded the retreat, and I ran. In truth, I would have run all the same, had the bugle not sounded. As I fled from the field, I was shot.

(A loud shot. JOSIAH cries out)

JOSIAH *(Reading)*
I tried my best to keep up, but the bullet had torn through my leg. I fell, unable to do much more than crawl. I was in this low position when a cannonball shattered the earth next to me. The explosion threw me into a river, and I soon lost consciousness. I awoke some time later, to find that the river had carried me to a strange harbor.

(Gunfire fades. The sound of frogs and crickets)

JOSIAH *(Reading)*
I determined I was in a bog, judging by the damp earth and foul smell. My time in the water had done nothing to remedy my leg. Mustering whatever reserves of strength I had, I crawled to a nearby hill in hopes of escaping whatever might be lurking in the swampland. Nearly senseless from the pain, I managed to set myself upon dry land. It was dusk, still light enough for me to see that my situation had improved only slightly. I had escaped the battlefield, only to find myself in a long-abandoned cemetery. Time and the rising waters had claimed much of it, but several grave markers still stood, like crooked teeth in a skull. It was against one of these headstones that I took my rest. The name upon it read "Abraham Cale." In my delirium, I laughed and asked Abraham to keep me company while I died. But Abraham did not come to me, nor did Death.

(Thunder and rain)

JOSIAH *(Reading)*
I lay on that morbid earth for days; I do not know how
many. The Spring rains kept me from dying of thirst, but
their passing brought a multitude of creatures to feast
and pester me.

(Sound of mosquitos)

JOSIAH *(Reading)*
The days ran together, and my time awake grew slight.
After perhaps the third day, I found the courage to
inspect my wounded leg. Oh, that I had not.

(The sound of wet cloth pulling away from rotten skin)

JOSIAH *(Reading)*
A foul smell worse than the swamp confirmed my
worst fears; the leg was gangrenous, a sickening rot
surrounding the wound. Had I my saber, I would have
attempted to remove the leg itself before the infection
spread upward, but I had lost it in the battle. I knew the
stories, I had seen the hospital tents. This putrescent
injury would kill me slowly, painfully, and there would
be no help. I prayed. I begged God to deliver me, to
send me any relief. But my weakness overtook me, and
I slipped back into oblivion. Upon awakening, I found
I was surrounded by mist, illuminated by moonlight.
A strange sense had roused me...a feeling that I was
not alone. And as I peered into the fog, my feeling was
confirmed. Drifting towards me was a woman, wrapped
in a dark mourning gown.

LARK
Do you live?

JOSIAH *(Reading)*
A voice like an angel. Had God heard my prayers?

LARK
Do you yet live, sir?

JOSIAH *(Reading)*
In my shock, I almost didn't respond.

JOSIAH
Help me. Please.

LARK
Rest easy. I won't hurt you.

JOSIAH
I am wounded.

JOSIAH *(Reading)*
And suddenly, she was there, kneeling down next to me. For a moment, I could not speak, for never in my life had I seen such beauty. Hair so dark that I could not tell where the night ended and she began. Eyes equally dark, set against a face so pale she seemed to glow under the stars. She reached out and touched my face.

LARK
Tell me. How are you hurt?

JOSIAH
My leg....shot...infected...

LARK
May I see it?

JOSIAH
No...please...it wouldn't be proper...

LARK
I have seen many such injuries, sir. I promise not to faint away.

(The sound of cloth peeling away from rotting skin.

JOSIAH *moans)*

LARK
Oh my. This is...oh my.

JOSIAH
I told you. There is nothing to be done.

LARK
You wear a soldier's uniform.

JOSIAH
I am a lieutenant.

LARK
You give up very quickly for a lieutenant.

JOSIAH
Well, unless you have a bone saw under your bodice...

(LARK laughs)

LARK
I must have forgotten it.

JOSIAH
Who are you? Why did you...?

LARK
My name is Lark.

JOSIAH
Lark?

LARK
Lark.

JOSIAH
Are you going to sing to me as I die?

LARK
Perhaps. Perhaps not.

JOSIAH
Here. There is a bullet loaded into this pistol, and the powder should be dry now.

LARK
No.

JOSIAH
If you want to help me, end my suffering.

LARK
Do you have nothing to live for? Your wife, your children...

JOSIAH
I am unwed, and have no one to mourn me.

LARK
A handsome man such as yourself? I find that hard to believe.

JOSIAH
It's true. I always believed...that when one finds love, true love, he knows it.

LARK
And you never found that love?

JOSIAH
I...no.

LARK
You must have dallied with local girls.

JOSIAH
That wouldn't be proper.

LARK
You are a true gentleman then?

JOSIAH
I was raised to treat a woman cordially. I cannot be that
but what I was raised to be.

(Pause)

LARK
Men like you are a rare breed.

JOSIAH
Come morning....there will be one less.

LARK
I can save you.

JOSIAH
I appreciate your concern, ma'am, but I'm a dead man
and nothing more.

LARK
You have to believe me. I am...I know how to stave off
this rot without removing the leg.

JOSIAH
Impossible.

LARK
I can do this. But you must trust me.

JOSIAH (Reading)
How was I to trust this woman I had just met? And yet,
the longer I stared into her dark eyes, the more I knew
I'd do anything she asked. She touched my face, and her
cool flesh took my fever from me. I could think clearly,
see clearly. I gasped.

LARK
What's wrong?

JOSIAH
I only...please forgive me, ma'am...

LARK
Lark.

JOSIAH
Lark, I...in my whole life, I believe I've never seen a woman so lovely.

LARK
That's the fever talking.

JOSIAH
It's the truth. I swear to it.

(Pause)

LARK
Then will you let me help you?

JOSIAH
I will.

LARK
You must know this my help comes at a price.

JOSIAH
I have no money. I left it at the camp and...

LARK
Not money. Something else.

JOSIAH
What?

LARK
I cannot tell you. You must accept this condition before I can help you.

JOSIAH
What do you want of me?

JOSIAH *(Reading)*
She did not answer with words. Instead she leaned in and kissed me, very softly. In that moment, I lost myself to her. If this was the price, I would pay it gladly.

LARK
Do you agree?

JOSIAH
I do.

LARK
Good. Thank you.

(Thunder sounds)

JOSIAH *(Reading)*
Lightning flashed nearby, and for a moment I could see nothing. When my vision returned, Lark was holding a flask before me.

JOSIAH
What is this?

LARK
Nothing to fear. Water, with a few drops of laudanum. You will sleep, and when you rise, your leg will be well again.

JOSIAH
Will...will you still be here?

LARK
Yes, dear heart. I will be here at your side.

JOSIAH *(Reading)*
And then she put the flask to my lips. I drank deep, and

slept deeper. How long I drifted in this slumber, I do not know. My dreams were troubled and strange, filled with buzzing flies and...and...

(Buzzing flies, and the sounds of chewing)

JOSIAH *(Reading)*
It was the sound of chewing, of teeth tearing through meat. Both sounds grew louder and louder...

(Buzzing and chewing increase in volume)

JOSIAH *(Reading)*
It seemed to be coming from all sides, inescapable. And with a start, I was awake. The cemetery was quiet and still. And then, the silence was broken by...

(The chewing resumes)

JOSIAH *(Reading)*
Dear god, the horrible sound had followed me out of my dream! I glanced about, but my eyes had not yet adjusted to the dark. Suddenly, the world was lit again by a flash of lightning and...

(More thunder)

JOSIAH *(Reading)*
What I saw that night has stayed with me, and I see it still, every day of my life. Lark, my beauteous savior, was bent over my leg. She must have heard my startled gasp, because she looked up at me. And...her porcelain skin ran red with blood. My blood. And in her mouth...my flesh. The diseased tissue of my leg hung like ribbons from her lips. She tried to say something, but filth poured out of her mouth.

(The sound of meat falling in the mud)

JOSIAH *(Reading)*
Panic seized me. I managed to scramble upright, my
hand searching for my pistol.

LARK
Wait! Please! Listen to me!

JOSIAH *(Reading)*
But I was beyond reason. I raised my weapon and fired.

(Gunshot)

JOSIAH *(Reading)*
My bullet found its mark, between her eyes. But she
did not fall. Instead, she stared at me, her face a mask
of unbearable sorrow. And suddenly...dear reader, what
happened next will strain credulity but you must know
that I write the truth, however horrid. *(Pause)* Lark's
body began to shake and shudder. And with a grotesque
lurch, the beautiful woman disappeared. Her body
became a mass of writhing maggots. I screamed, for what
else could I do? And then, she collapsed into herself,
hundreds...thousands of the vile worms falling to the
earth below.

(A wet noise of falling maggots)

JOSIAH *(Reading)*
All reason left me, and I ran. My only sense was to run
away from the water, to whatever dry land I could find.
But behind me, I could hear Lark...or whatever this
creature was that called itself by that name.

LARK
I love you! I will love you always!

JOSIAH *(Reading)*
I raced against the sound.

LARK
Don't leave me, Husband! Stay with me!

JOSIAH *(Reading)*
I ran with renewed speed.

LARK
You are mine!

JOSIAH *(Reading)*
I rushed through the cemetery, into the woods beyond. It was at least an hour before I realized that I should not have been able to run at all. Resting against a large willow, I looked at my leg. It bled, to be sure, but all traces of the wet rot were gone. The befouled flesh had disappeared, and the healthy flesh remained. I ripped my sleeve open, and wrapped it around the wound.

(Sound of cloth ripping)

JOSIAH *(Reading)*
My injury bound, I continued my escape through the forest. The sun rose, and I saw before me a small town. I staggered towards it, my mind reeling from the events of the night before. I finally collapsed in the street, no longer able to think or even move. I came to several hours later to find a bespectacled old man looking at me.

DOCTOR
There now, son. You just rest.

JOSIAH
Where am I...

DOCTOR
A little town called Cully's Holler. My name's John Winslow, and I'm the one patching up this leg of yours.

JOSIAH
A doctor?

DOCTOR
Best one in town. Also the only one in town. Now do
me a favor and bite down on this.

JOSIAH *(Reading)*
He put a leather strap in my mouth.

DOCTOR
Go ahead and bite down good. This is gonna smart.

*(The sound of pouring liquid. JOSIAH cries out through
gritted teeth)*

DOCTOR
Had to be done. That alcohol's gonna keep this hole
from getting infected. I'm surprised it hasn't been yet.
Shot in the battle, were ya?

JOSIAH *(Reading)*
I related to the doctor my escape from the battle of
Shiloh, and how I found myself in the cemetery just
outside of town. I did not tell him of my night with...
whatever she was. But I did ask him if he knew of a
woman named...

DOCTOR
Lark? Well, not exactly. Closest would've been Larkin
Cale, I reckon.

JOSIAH
Who is she? Where is she?

DOCTOR
Who she is is the wife of the doctor before me. Where
she is is that very cemetery you run out of. She's been
dead goin' on twenty years now.

JOSIAH
What?

DOCTOR
It's a hell of a story. You wanna hear it?

JOSIAH
I do. Very much.

DOCTOR
Well, Larkin was married to old Abraham Cale. Vicious son of a bitch. He was a doctor to some, but most called him a butcher instead. See, old Abe was a drinker and a mean drunk too. He even took a nip or five when he was doin' surgery. Well, turns out his pretty wife was a quick study and sometimes helped him treat the sick. Some say that the only reason he didn't get rode out was 'cause Larkin kept alive them that Abraham made worse. Well like I said, he was a cruel bastard. Didn't like that people thought better of his wife than they did of him. He'd beat her...

(The sound of a hard slap. LARK cries out)

DOCTOR
...and he'd have his way with her in a real ungentle-manly way.

(Tearing cloth. LARK cries out again)

LARK
NO!

DOCTOR
Well, one day Lark is healing up a man got run over by a cart. Caleb Gurney. He'd waited too long to get his foot looked at, and it started to turn. She was doin' what most doctors don't do no more...usin' maggots.

JOSIAH
What?

DOCTOR
Oh, it's a good treatment. See, maggots...they eat rotten flesh, but they leave the good. It ain't pretty to look at, but it's real effective. Anyway, old Abraham comes home drunker than a waltzing piss ant. He sees his wife doin' what he figures is his job, and starts to beat her something awful. Caleb tries to stop him, but he can't get about real good on his bad foot. By the time he pulled Abraham off Larkin, it was too late. He'd cracked her head open. Well, they strung up old Abe for it, not that it done the poor Maggot Woman any good.

JOSIAH
What did you call her?

DOCTOR
Oh. The Maggot Woman. Just a name some of the young'ns round here gave her. Caleb said she kept a big jar full of the wrigglers, just to help out people like him.

JOSIAH *(Reading)*
The old doctor tended my wound, but my mind reeled from the story he told me. In a week I was well enough to leave, and I put as much distance between me and Cully's Holler as I could. But his story haunts me still, and will for the rest of my life. Because I know now. I know what the price for her healing is.

(He pours a drink, drinks it)

JOSIAH *(Reading)*
At night, I sometimes feel them. The maggots, crawling underneath my skin. I have taken a knife to my flesh countless times, but every time I do, they stop. She healed the wound in my leg, but the price....

LARK
Stay with me!

JOSIAH *(Reading)*
I know with great certainty what awaits me when I die.

LARK
Don't leave me, Husband.

JOSIAH *(Reading)*
They will lay my body in the ground. Over time, the worms and maggots will consume me. And then...they will become my flesh.

LARK
I love you.

JOSIAH *(Reading)*
Don't ask me how I know this. Just trust that it is true.

LARK
I will love you always.

JOSIAH *(Reading)*
When Josiah Walker finally dies...when his body becomes food for the worms...

LARK
You are mine.

JOSIAH *(Reading)*
...then the Maggot Woman will finally have a new husband.

THE END

A MODEL SON

(1970s-era rock & roll plays on a radio, something horror-themed perhaps. A knock on the door)

LINDA
Tommy?

(He turns the music off)

TOMMY
I'm not here.

LINDA
Then who turned off the radio? And answered me?

TOMMY
Leave me alone, Mom.

LINDA
We need to talk.

TOMMY
Later!

LINDA
Five, four...

TOMMY
Mom!

LINDA
...three, two...

TOMMY
(Muttering to himself) Goddammit.

LINDA
...One.

(The door opens)

LINDA
Oh my goodness! Tommy!

TOMMY
What?

LINDA
That smell...what is that?

TOMMY
I don't know. Methylbenzene, toluol, phenylmethane probably.

LINDA
It's that model glue, isn't it?

TOMMY
That's what I said.

LINDA
Well, open the window, for pete's sake!

TOMMY
I'm fine.

LINDA
You're not fine. You're up here breathing those fumes

and... Tommy.

TOMMY
Mom.

LINDA
I'm concerned.

TOMMY
Don't be.

LINDA
This monster phase...it's got to end.

TOMMY
It's not a phase. It's me.

LINDA
The posters, the masks, all these models...

TOMMY
They're mine. I bought them with my allowance.

LINDA
Remind me. Where do you get your allowance from?

(Pause)

TOMMY
What do you want, Mom?

LINDA
Your father and I have been talking...

TOMMY
When the neighbors can hear you, it's not talking. It's shouting.

LINDA
I've had just about enough of your lip, mister. We, your father and I, we...

(CARL yells from downstairs)

CARL
You tell him to go outside already?!

LINDA
(Yelling back) I'm talking to him now!

CARL
Don't you shout at me! You got that?

LINDA
Your father and I think you should maybe get some fresh air. Outside.

TOMMY
Really? I'd never have guessed.

LINDA
Maybe go Christmas shopping, or see a movie with your friends or...

TOMMY
I'm all set, thanks.

LINDA
It's just...you spend so much time in here, with these creepy things. Don't you want to get out of here? Enjoy life a little?

TOMMY
I am enjoying life! These models...they're little worlds I create. I follow the instructions, and make something beautiful and perfect and...

LINDA
Dr. Colson says you're hiding; that you're having a hard time in the real world and you're looking for something you can control.

TOMMY
You see this? This is Aurora's newest Monster Scenes Model. Dr. Deadly.

LINDA
Which movie is it from?

TOMMY
He's not from any movie! He's an original character, created by Aurora.

LINDA
He looks like Peter Lorre.

TOMMY
I thought more like a fat Vincent Price, but...look. This makes me happy. Painting these models, reading these magazines, watching old horror movies makes me happy.

LINDA
But you get that it's...a little odd, right?

TOMMY
I don't care! Just 'cause you and dad are miserable, don't expect me to follow suit!

LINDA
(Calling off to CARL) Carl! Talk to your son!

CARL
I'm watching Hee Haw, goddammit! Tell that little shitstain he's going outside through the front door, or through the window! His choice!

LINDA
Tommy, you have ten minutes to finish up painting that...thing, then get out of this tomb. God, these fumes are just killing my head...

(She exits, slamming the door)

TOMMY
Ok, Dr. Deadly. Let's just set you right in the Pain Parlor
while I find some glow paint...

(The sounds of lab equipment start)

DR. DEADLY
No, my boy. There will be no need for that.

(Pause)

TOMMY
Dad?

DR. DEADLY
Do I sound like that beer-swilling waste of flesh?

TOMMY
...no?...

DR. DEADLY
Look around. I'm closer than you think.

(TOMMY opens the closet door)

DR. DEADLY
The closet, Tommy? Really? Why not check under the
bed while you're at it?

(TOMMY upends his bed)

DR. DEADLY
I didn't...that was a joke.

TOMMY
Who the hell is it? No one's allowed in my room but me!

DR. DEADLY
Allowed? Tommy, you brought me here yourself!

(Pause)

TOMMY
Doc...Doctor Deadly?

(The sound of an electric current)

DR. DEADLY
That's my boy! That's my bright, bespectacled boy!

TOMMY
Oh man...I'm talking to a...holy shit. Have I gone nuts?

DR. DEADLY
I don't like to make those sorts of judgments. Besides, my degree isn't in psychology.

TOMMY
You're just a model.

DR. DEADLY
A model of scientific achievement, perhaps. And now that you've given me a happy home, and thank you for that, I can truly begin my good work. But...Tommy, may I speak frankly?

TOMMY
I don't know how you're speaking at all.

DR. DEADLY
I look at you and I see the assistant I've always dreamed of.

TOMMY
Really?

DR. DEADLY
Oh, absolutely. Bright, imaginative, passionate...but I worry that your heart won't be in the work.

TOMMY
It will! I promise! Look at my room! Monsters are my

life!

DR. DEADLY
Yes, but they're not your entire life, are they?

(Pause)

TOMMY
What do you mean?

DR. DEADLY
You're still very young. A boy, really. And a boy needs his parents.

TOMMY
My parents are bogue.

DR. DEADLY
Perhaps, but bogueness aside, I know how much you love them. It hurts you when they fight, doesn't it?

TOMMY
Yeah.

DR. DEADLY
Would you like to help them stop fighting? Forever?

(The sound of a blade chopping into wood)

DR. DEADLY
Oops! Looks like that guillotine is a little twitchy. Could you pass me some adhesive?

(The sound of DR. DEADLY working on the guillotine)

DR. DEADLY
Now, as I was saying…Tommy, I want to help you. I want you to all be one big, happy family again.

TOMMY
Can you build a time machine? 'Cause that's what it

would take.

DR. DEADLY
My work tends to be more...biological than mechanical.
But don't let that discourage you. I can help you, all of
you. I really can.

TOMMY
How?

DR. DEADLY
Well, what time do you eat dinner tomorrow?

TOMMY
Um...Six O'Clock. Why?

DR. DEADLY
Could you set a fourth place at the table? I'd like to have
a word with your parents.

*(The sound of a ticking clock, perhaps bells tolling six.
Time passes. It's the next day)*

LINDA
Tommy? Sweetie? Dinner!

CARL
He's not gonna come down if...TOMMY! Get your ass
down here double time!

TOMMY
I'm coming!

CARL
This meatloaf isn't gonna eat itself!

LINDA
You don't have to yell at him.

CARL
I could do a lot worse than yelling. Remember that.

(The sound of TOMMY running down the stairs)

CARL
Oh, what the hell is this?

TOMMY
What?

LINDA
Tommy, you know the rule. No toys at the table.

TOMMY
He's not a toy. He's a doctor.

CARL
You want me to smash it? 'Cause I'll smash it.

TOMMY
I wouldn't.

(Pause)

CARL
Did you just threaten me?

LINDA
No, he didn't. Let's just…meatloaf's ready! Tommy, put the toy on the floor.

DR. DEADLY
I'm not a toy, woman! I'm…

TOMMY
OK, mom.

LINDA
Let's say grace. Bless you, heavenly father, for this meal and this family and…

CARL
Yeah, yeah, yeah. Pass the ketchup.

(CARL pours ketchup on his meal)

LINDA
Honey, you're drowning it.

CARL
Swimming in ketchup is the only way I can eat this crap.
Know what? That's how you're gonna eat it too.

(He covers her food in ketchup)

LINDA
Carl, that's too much...

CARL
You smartin' off to me? Are you?

LINDA
...no...

CARL
Good. Let's eat.

(The sound of the family eating)

DR. DEADLY
Look at them, shoveling food into their mouths like
swine. Where's the civility? Where's the discussion?
Where's the love? That's what I want to know, Tommy.

TOMMY
Quiet.

DR. DEADLY
Where's the love?

CARL
What was that?

TOMMY
I wasn't talking to you.

DR. DEADLY
Plebeian.

LINDA
Tommy, don't get smart with your father.

TOMMY
Of course not! God forbid I actually say anything at all!
You two might have to stop fighting for two seconds!

DR. DEADLY
Ha! Well said, my boy!

CARL
Hey! That's your mother! Don't you...!

TOMMY
What?! Don't what?! Christ! Could you just...could you
both just stop shouting for two minutes and listen to
me?! PLEASE?!

(Awkward silence)

DR. DEADLY
Go on, Tommy. Say what you need to say.

TOMMY
We used to be happy. Remember that? We used to be so
happy, all of us. Dad, you dressed up as Santa and we sang
carols and...I don't know what happened. I don't know
if you hate me now or...

LINDA
Tommy...

TOMMY
Let me say this, ok. I just...I love you guys. I love you so
much and I know that...I know you're getting a divorce.

CARL
Well, now...

TOMMY
Am I wrong? Because I was outside your door last night. You said the word "divorce" sixteen times. So tell me... am I wrong?

(Pause)

LINDA
Honey, sometimes things change as we get older. It doesn't mean we don't love you; it just...

TOMMY
Stop. Please. Let me say this.

DR. DEADLY
I'm here, Tommy. I'm right here.

TOMMY
It's so stupid...I should've said this a long time ago. I guess...I guess I needed Dr. Deadly to give me the courage to...

CARL
Doctor...Deadly?

TOMMY
Here, let me just put him on the table. He and I have been talking and...I don't want you to split up. I want us to be a family again. I love you. I need you here, with me.

(CARL starts to cough a bit)

CARL
Kid, just 'cause we're not gonna be living together doesn't mean...

LINDA
Let me get you some water. That's what happens when you eat too fast.

TOMMY
That's not what it is.

LINDA
What?

TOMMY
Like I said, Dr. Deadly and I have been talking. Turns out he's as good at chemistry as I am. But he's way more creative. I'm gonna learn so much from him.

DR. DEADLY
Son, it will be my pleasure.

TOMMY
And we both kind of realized...you two will never stay together. Not willingly. And we'll never be that happy family that I remember when I was little.

LINDA
Tommy...?

(LINDA starts to cough too)

TOMMY
Not without my help.

CARL
I can't....my legs...I can't move...

TOMMY
That's a lead-based poison. I put it in the ketchup. Turns out some of the stuff in model paint is really toxic.

LINDA
Oh god! Tommy...

(Her coughing overtakes her)

DR. DEADLY
Tell them not to worry.

TOMMY
Don't worry. It will pass. Well, the coughing will pass. And then, you will.

(The sound of furniture/plates falling)

TOMMY
I'm going to do what you should've done. I'm going to make us a real family. I'm sorry it had to come to this. I am. But trust me, things are gonna be so much better now. I'm a good son, and I'm going to make good parents out of you.

(His parents fall to the floor)

DR. DEADLY
I do believe they're dead, Tommy.

TOMMY
I know.

DR. DEADLY
Shall we get to work?

(The ticking clock again. Time passes)

DR. DEADLY
You see? Who needs plastic and model glue when you can create in flesh and blood?

TOMMY
I wish you could've helped. Getting them set up on the couch took forever.

DR. DEADLY
But look at them! Arms around each other, Christmas

gifts all around…it's a perfect scene of familial love!

TOMMY
It gets better.

(The sound of cloth being shaken)

DR. DEADLY
Your father's Santa costume!

TOMMY
It was in the attic! I couldn't believe he still had it.

DR. DEADLY
Time to add the finishing touch to your greatest model ever.

TOMMY
Thank you, good doctor. I agree completely.

(Sound of TOMMY struggling)

DR. DEADLY
Having some trouble?

TOMMY
Rigor mortis set in. I can't move his arms.

DR. DEADLY
Damn. That's a fly in the ointment.

TOMMY
What am I gonna do? I need to put him in the Santa outfit. I need to!

DR. DEADLY
Well, I have an…unorthodox solution.

TOMMY
Yeah?

DR. DEADLY
I noticed your father's tool kit in the living room closet.

TOMMY
So?

DR. DEADLY
Is there perhaps…a saw inside?

TOMMY
Oh! Let me check!

(TOMMY empties the tool kit)

TOMMY
Found one!

DR. DEADLY
Then let's get to work!

(The sound of sawing through skin, muscle and bone)

TOMMY
Man! This is really tough. Getting through the bone is…

DR. DEADLY
You can do it, Tommy! Where there's a will and a hand saw, there's a way!

(More sawing. The arm falls off)

DR. DEADLY
Well done! Now you can slip it right into the sleeve and position it wherever you want it.

TOMMY
I'm thinking one arm around mom, the other holding some mistletoe over her head. What do you think?

DR. DEADLY
They're your parents. Whatever you decide will be lovely.

TOMMY
Thanks, Dr. Deadly. You're the best.

DR. DEADLY
Though might I suggest crossing your mother's legs? It might make her look less...wanton.

TOMMY
Good idea. Lemme just...come on, you stupid knee... just give already...

(The sound of bones snapping)

TOMMY
There! Finally! Just cross the left leg over the right and...Perfect!

DR. DEADLY
Now, let us plug in the tree, turn on the record player, and marvel at this scene of holiday bliss.

(Some Christmas music starts to play)

TOMMY
You know what, Doc?

DR. DEADLY
What's that?

TOMMY
This is gonna be the best Christmas ever.

(They sing along with the music)

THE END

APPLE BOBBERS

(The sound of people talking and general teenage party noises. A great deal of splashing is heard as kids cheer. We hear BECKY and JENNA gasp for air as they raise their heads from the water basin)

BECKY
YES! YES! Eight! Eight mother–fudging apples!

JENNA
Oh gosh...it's in my nose...

BECKY
Jenna! You didn't get a single apple?

JENNA
(Coughing) ...couldn't...felt like I was...drowning...

BECKY
Ugh, you're such a little chicken.

JENNA
...I could see Jesus...

BECKY
Well, that means…I WIN!

(Kids cheer)

BECKY
I am the undefeated apple bobbing champion! Bow down before me, y'all!

JENNA
Towel…need towel…

BECKY
Here.

(She dries off JENNA and herself)

BECKY
Now, if you're not too scared of fluids, I'm gonna get us some cider.

(BECKY collides with KIM. The sound of spilled drinks)

BECKY
Ow! Dangit all!

KIM
Come on! You made me spill my…!

BECKY
Is this your first time walking? Honestly. I'm asking you.

JENNA
Nice one, Becky.

KIM
Goddammit, it's all over my…

BECKY
Excuse me? Do you even know where you are?

KIM
My own personal hell?

BECKY
This is a church! You just watch that pierced tongue of yours!

KIM
You sound like a mom.

BECKY
My mother is a strong, beautiful, and HOLY woman, so thank you.

(Pause)

KIM
I'm gonna go now.

BECKY
Look at her. All tramped up like that. Black fingernails, black lipstick...

JENNA
I think she looks hot...

(BECKY glares at her)

JENNA
...Topic is probably where she bought those clothes.

BECKY
So trashy. Why is she even here?

JENNA
Because you invited her?

BECKY
My momma said I had to! You know she lives with her grandma, right?

JENNA
Yeah, I heard her folks are weed-pushers.

BECKY
Oh, they soooo are. So when they got busted, poor little Kim Smith had to move in with her grandma. Anyway, my momma says her grandma just had a stroke...Kim's, not my momma's...and so here she is. There's Christian kindness for ya.

JENNA
Well, and she helped with the party.

BECKY
Pffft. "Helped." She like got some of the decorations and food and stuff. I'm the one that's been here all day, settin' up the Salem Witch Bonfire and the Horrors of Evolution House and...

JENNA
This place looks great, Becky.

BECKY
Thank you! And isn't my costume just the cutest thing ever?

JENNA
It's...real short.

BECKY
It has to be short! I'm a sexy pizza! But it still leaves somethin' to the imagination. Hence, the strategically placed pepperonis.

JENNA
I don't...how is pizza sexy?

BECKY
Um, the sauce. 'Cause it's saucy.

JENNA
Oh.

BECKY
But then Princess of Darkness Kim shows up and no one's even lookin' at me! And you know why, don't you?

JENNA
Well, she's got this kinda "forbidden fruit" thing goin' on and...

BECKY
I heard that she...goes all the way.

JENNA
No!

BECKY
Yes! And she's not even wearing a costume! This is the last time I help out someone in need, I swear.

(A clock chimes)

BECKY
Oh shoot...*(She addresses the crowd)* Y'all! Hush up, y'all!

(The crowd quiets down)

BECKY
Y'all, I wanna thank you all for comin' on out to Midland First Baptist's tenth annual Hallelujahween Party...

JENNA
Halloween-ed be thy name!

BECKY
This year, all the money we raise is goin' to help fund our Youth Ministry trip to Guada...Guaca...

JENNA
Guadalajara.

BECKY
So go on and give give give!

(The crowd cheers)

BECKY
And in about ten minutes, we're gonna start the Articles
of Faith Pumpkin Carving Contest!

(She claps with excitement)

BECKY
So enjoy some pizza and soda and...

(Murmuring in the crowd. BECKY talks to JENNA)

BECKY
Jenna. JENNA! What's goin' on?

JENNA
I think...that's a cop!

BECKY
But we haven't done anything! Hold on...

(BECKY pushes her way through the crowd to MASON)

BECKY
...'scuse me...I'm sorry, 'scuse me, just...Sir? SIR?! Is
somethin' the matter?

MASON
Miss, is your mother here?

BECKY
No, I'm in charge.

MASON
Aren't you a little young for...?

BECKY
I'm 18!

MASON
I'm looking for a Kimberly Irene Smith. She here?

BECKY
Oh son of a biscuit! I should've known! That's her, offi-cer. The tramp in the jeans so tight they look like a tattoo!

MASON
(Calling to KIM) Miss? I need a word.

JENNA
What's goin' on?

BECKY
I'm bettin' Kim's selling weed here or...

KIM
What's up?

MASON
I'm Dr. Mason with the Center for Disease Control. Would you please come with me?

KIM
No.

MASON
I'm afraid I'm going to have to insist.

KIM
You a cop?

MASON
No, I'm a doctor.

KIM
Then fuck off.

BECKY
Kim!

KIM
I'm just here to have a good time. I haven't done anything wrong.

(In the background, people start to cough)

MASON
I need to speak with you about your grandmother.

KIM
Granny's a sweet old lady stuck in a wheelchair. You leave her alone!

MASON
She's in custody now, but...

KIM
You cocksuckers!

(KIM strikes MASON)

KIM
She just wanted to be left alone! Why can't y'all just leave us alone!? Just 'cause we're backwoods don't mean you can just...just...!

(Water splashes as KIM grabs the water basin)

BECKY
Put that down! We're gonna do more apple bobbing later!

KIM
Bob this!

(She hurls the water and apples at the crowd. They respond)

KIM
Yeah, drink up, holy-rollers!

JENNA
Stop it!

(KIM sings as she throws water/apples)

KIM
Don't sit under the apple tree with anyone else but me...

MASON
Please, just come with me...

KIM
Hey! Get your fucking hands off me!

BECKY
What...what's going on?

JENNA
Wait! Center for Disease Control!? That...like is there an outbreak or...

MASON
Miss, I need you to tell me what your grandmother did!

KIM
Y'all make fun of Granny and me 'cause we're poor! Every Halloween, punk ass kids tear up her lawn and egg our house and...

MASON
We don't have time for this!

(BECKY coughs a little. The background coughing gets worse)

MASON
We traced the contamination back to your grandmother's house, but she can't talk! We need you to tell us what she put on those apples!

BECKY
...apples?

MASON
We found her room in the attic, the one full of all that...
stuff and...

KIM
You mean Granny's hoodoo room?

(The coughing around grows)

KIM
Yeah, turns out we're not all Baptists 'round here.

BECKY
What did you do!?

MASON
People are dying! Do you get that!? People who bought
apples from you are dying all over this city!

JENNA
Dying!?

BECKY
Oh...oh gosh...I feel...

KIM
Let 'em die! Sanctimonious assholes!

BECKY
...language...

JENNA
Becky, you look funny.

(BECKY begins to convulse)

MASON
How do we stop it?!

JENNA
Stop what?

KIM
You can't.

JENNA
STOP WHAT!?

KIM
Granny cursed those apples. CDC don't have a cure for curses, does it?

MASON
There's no such thing as...

(Screams in the background)

BECKY
What's...happening to...

(BECKY's scream becomes oddly liquid. The sound of a human body liquefying)

JENNA
HOLY SHIT! BECKY!!

MASON
What's happening to her?!

KIM
She's melting.

JENNA
What!?

KIM
Criss-cross applesauce.

(BECKY's scream is cut short as she plops to the ground, a liquid pile of human soup)

JENNA
Oh...oh sweet merciful god...

(JENNA vomits)

MASON
You have to stop this!

KIM
Yeah? Why?

(In the background, more people begin to liquefy)

JENNA
Becky...oh Becky...you're all...soup.

KIM
You bastards spit on me and mine for too fuckin' long!

(MASON gets on a walkie-talkie)

MASON
Base, this is Mason. We need all trucks at Midland First Baptist NOW!

KIM
Granny and I put a little somethin'-somethin' on each and every one of them apples! Trick or treat! Trick or fuckin' treat!

(The screams around grow louder)

MASON
(To JENNA) C'mon, miss. We need to get you to the trucks.

JENNA
I didn't eat any of the apples! *(Pause. JENNA laughs with joy)* Holy shit! I didn't eat any! YES! FUCK YES! I'm gonna live!

KIM
Funny story...

JENNA
I'M GONNA LIVE!!!

KIM
Curse works on the water too.

JENNA
Hmmm?

KIM
Any water the apples touch gets cursed too.

MASON
BASE! ETA ON THE GODDAMN TRUCKS!

KIM
Me, I'm safe. Granny worked her magic good. But the rest of y'all?

(JENNA begins to cough and convulse)

KIM
Criss. Cross. Applesauce.

JENNA
No...oh god no...I feel...I feel...

KIM
Bet you're glad you wore that space-suit, CDC.

(JENNA screams and liquefies)

KIM
There she goes.

(People are liquefying around them. MASON snaps hand-cuffs on KIM)

KIM
Hey! What's this shit?

MASON
I'm taking you in.

KIM
What kinda doctor has handcuffs?!

MASON
Prepared ones. C'mon.

KIM
Hippopotamus oath, man! You gotta save these people!

MASON
With what? Anti-curse vaccine? Hoodoo-cilin?

KIM
Get off me!

MASON
I can't stop this, but I can stop you. I...oh, shit. I think
I just stepped in...teenager.

KIM
Bad apples! That's what my granny called all y'all...bad
apples!

MASON
Oh god...I'm going to be sick.

(KIM laughs as MASON drags her off)

KIM
Bad apples for bad apples! BAD APPLES FOR BAD
APPLES!

THE END

BAD TEETH

(A cell door slams shut)

KIM
How you doin', Etta? Bad? You doin' bad?

(ETTA moans)

KIM
Let's just check those restraints, yeah?

ETTA
What...what you doin'...?

KIM
Hey! Look who's awake!

ETTA
...where am I...?

KIM
So here's the thing, Etta. Everyone on your cellblock's been talking. Know why?

ETTA
...why you tie me down?

KIM
'Cause you stink, sister. The warden herself says your breath smells like you ate the ass end out of a dead hog. So guess who's getting a little dental work today. It's you, you old bitch!

ETTA
No...no no no...

KIM
OK. Looks like you're strapped in good.

(Buzz of a walkie-talkie turning on)

KIM
The prisoner is secure. You can send the doctor in.

(The cell door opens and closes)

KIM
Heya. You must be Dr. Billings.

BILLINGS
That's right.

KIM
Kim LeMarque. I'm gonna be here today, just keeping an eye on things.

BILLINGS
Pleased to meet you, officer.

KIM
Oh, "Kim" is fine.

BILLINGS
Kim, did...um...did Warden Hollis explain to you the... um...

KIM
Oh, she told me everything. Don't you worry, Doc. What

happens in Med Room #4 stays in Med Room #4.

BILLINGS
Thank you.

KIM
De nada. This sick fuck? I say go to town.

(KIM strikes ETTA)

KIM
Hey! You still with us, killer? I know they sedated you before, but...

BILLINGS
Not too much. I need her to feel this.

KIM
Oh, she's already coming out of it. Aren't you?

ETTA
Why you keep hitting me?

KIM
I don't know. Spirit just moved me, I guess.

(KIM strikes ETTA again)

KIM
Lookit that! It moved me again. OK, Dr. Ellie Billings, meet Etta Mae Bodine. The Canton Cannibal. I'd tell you her resume, but I get the impression that you know it pretty well, yeah?

BILLINGS
Yes. Very well.

ETTA
Please don't hit me no more.

BILLINGS
God, her mouth is just...

KIM
Oh yeah. Look at them rotten snaggleteeth. What do you wanna bet this hillbilly hasn't brushed since never?

BILLINGS
I imagine her diet didn't help.

KIM
You're the doctor.

BILLINGS
Yes, I am.

(The sound of BILLINGS laying out various equipment)

ETTA
Why...why you got all that?

BILLINGS
Well, Ms. Bodine, it looks as though you're going to require some very significant dental work. I'm here to do that.

ETTA
I ain't doped up no more.

BILLINGS
No, you're not. And you won't be.

ETTA
What?

KIM
Jeez, Doc. That's some old school shit you've got there.

BILLINGS
You like this? This is a vintage 1950 Emesco 90-N dental drill. It's rusty, and it's dull, but it will get the job done.

(She revs the drill)

ETTA
You keep that thing away from me!

BILLINGS
The only thing I seem to have forgotten is the Novocain.

ETTA
You can't cut me! You hear?! I got the darkness inside me! You can't...!

(BILLINGS puts her hand over ETTA's mouth)

BILLINGS
Listen to me, you sick piece of trash. I'm going to cut you. I'm going to pull and slice and drill and there's not a damn thing you can do about it. Those people you hurt... I'm going to give you a fraction of what you did to them.

KIM
Shit, I say shove that old drill into her brain and call it a night.

BILLINGS
I'm not going to kill her. I won't sink to her level. I'm not...

KIM
Lord, don't get maudlin. Just make this bitch scream.

BILLINGS
Yes. Good idea.

ETTA
You gotta listen! I got the darkness! If you hurt me, the darkness come out! I don't wanna hurt nobody! Just stay away!

(The sound of struggling as they shove a brace into ETTA's mouth)

BILLINGS
Considering your penchant for eating people, I thought it might be best to bring a Jennings Gag. It may be old, and it may taste it, but it'll keep you from biting down. I'll be walking out of this room with all my fingers.

(ETTA makes unintelligible noise)

BILLINGS
Feel free to scream, Ms. Bodine. Trust me, you're going to want to scream. Now let's take a look.

(She pokes and prods, provoking pained noises from ETTA)

BILLINGS
Oooooh yeah. Yeah, this is bad. There's significant decay in every single tooth. I don't think I've ever seen anything quite like it. Was the patient a smoker?

KIM
No, but she had a packet of chaw in her jeans when we brought her in.

BILLINGS
Tobacco? Tsk, tsk, tsk.

(ETTA makes unintelligible noise)

BILLINGS
Well, there's nothing for it. I can see at least...two, three, four...there's at least five teeth that have to go immediately. You see that molar there?

KIM
Mm-hmm.

BILLINGS
That's maybe savable, but it's going to need a root canal. Now.

(ETTA makes unintelligible noise. BILLINGS revs the drill)

BILLINGS
No point in struggling, Ms. Bodine. This is happening.

(The sound of tooth-drilling. ETTA screams)

BILLINGS
Jenny. Weatherly. Does that name sound familiar?

(More drilling and screaming)

BILLINGS
I imagine you didn't bother to learn the names of your victims, but one of them was JENNY...

(More drilling and screaming)

BILLINGS
WEATHERLY!

(More drilling and screaming)

BILLINGS
My niece. Ten years old. A ten year old girl who...she never...Fuck you, Bodine! You goddamn...!

(More drilling and screaming)

BILLINGS
Scream! Scream like she screamed!

KIM
Get in there, Doc! Put your shoulder into it!

(The drilling stops)

KIM
Damn. Was just getting good.

BILLINGS
She's close to passing out. Could you hand me my bag?

KIM
Sure. What'cha need?

BILLINGS
I brought an adrenaline shot. I want her awake for every second of this.

(She digs through the bag)

KIM
Christ. That's one big-ass needle.

BILLINGS
You're not wrong.

(The sound of the needle jamming into ETTA)

BILLINGS
There. That should keep her up.

(BILLINGS slaps ETTA. She moans)

BILLINGS
Come back, Etta. We're not done yet. Not by a long shot.

KIM
Heh. Shot.

(She clinks some pliers together)

BILLINGS
Drilling out the rotten nerve wasn't enough. Time to pull this thing out by the roots.

KIM
Now we're talking.

(ETTA makes unintelligible noises of protest)

BILLINGS
Kim, would you mind holding down her head? She's going to thrash and...

KIM
Hey, I'm just happy to be part of the team.

BILLINGS
Good. Very good. Now open wide, Ms. Bodine. Not that you have a choice. This is going to hurt. A lot.

(BILLINGS starts to pull. ETTA starts to scream)

KIM
Got some trouble there, Doc?

BILLINGS
I don't...it's not coming out...

(She strains to pull. ETTA screams)

KIM
Put some muscle into it!

BILLINGS
I don't understand! It's like the damn tooth is hooked in her jawbone! Come on...COME ON!!!

(ETTA screams loudly. BILLINGS gets the tooth out)

BILLINGS
Jesus, that was really in there.

KIM
God, lookit that thing. Like a sick old tree.

(ETTA moans)

BILLINGS
That was just the first tooth, Ms. Bodine. When I'm done with you, your mouth will be a ruined, festering wreck. I'm going to...

(The sound of a thick, viscous fluid oozing/spraying out of ETTA's mouth. BILLINGS & KIM cough and gag)

KIM
Holy shit!

BILLINGS
Oh my god…

KIM
Jesus…is that blood?!

BILLINGS
I don't…I'm not sure! I…!

KIM
She got black goop pouring out of her gums! What else could it be?

BILLINGS
Blood doesn't smell like that! This is like oil or sludge or…

KIM
Doc. Doc.

BILLINGS
What?!

KIM
It's moving.

BILLINGS
WHAT?

KIM
Look at it! It's…it's slithering out of her mouth! It's moving and growing and…

(A strange, alien moaning)

BILLINGS
Did…did that stuff just…moan?

KIM
Time to go.

DARKNESS
Huuuuuuuuuuuuuuuuungry....

BILLINGS
Oh god...

DARKNESS
HUUUUUNGRY!

BILLINGS
Kim! Look out!

(A slurping sound as the DARKNESS attacks KIM. She cries out)

BILLINGS
Kim!? Are you...?!

KIM
Goddamn thing....broke my arms...

(The DARKNESS moans)

KIM
Doc...you gotta get...my walkie...

BILLINGS
I'm not going near that thing.

KIM
It's gonna kill us unless you...

DARKNESS
HUNGRY!

KIM
Fuck! Keep away from me!

DARKNESS
Need....to...EAT!

KIM
Please! Please god just leave me alone!

DARKNESS
...Hurt...friend!

KIM
I didn't! It was her! The doctor!

DARKNESS
HURT FRIEND!

BILLINGS
Listen...Listen to me! Whatever you are...you don't
have to hurt us!

DARKNESS
Need food...hurt friend...

BILLINGS
We didn't...your friend...is a very bad woman.

DARKNESS
Etta is...friend...

BILLINGS
Can you tell us what you are? What you...?

DARKNESS
Old.

BILLINGS
What?

DARKNESS
I am...old.

BILLINGS
You're old. All right. That's….how old are you?

DARKNESS
Oldest. Nothing is…older.

KIM
Stop talking to it! Just…

BILLINGS
Do you have a name?

DARKNESS
Older than names.

BILLINGS
All right. We can still…

DARKNESS
Live inside Etta. Live inside many before Etta.

BILLINGS
What do you want from us?

KIM
Don't ask it that!

BILLINGS
If we can reason with it…

DARKNESS
FOOD! Need food! Must….eat…must eat…or must sleep…No more sleep…Must eat life…all life…YOU!

KIM
No! NO NO NO! Stay away! I got kids!

DARKNESS
FOOD!

KIM
I do Toys for Tots every year! Please! Don't...!

DARKNESS
FOOOOOOD!

BILLINGS
Oh, god!

(KIM cries out. The sound of a body being torn apart, devoured)

BILLINGS
Kim...Jesus Christ...

DARKNESS
Hurt Etta...no more...

BILLINGS
You...you killed her.

DARKNESS
Needed food.

BILLINGS
Please...I'm begging you...don't hurt me.

DARKNESS
Must...hide...

BILLINGS
I don't understand.

DARKNESS
Air...burns...light burns...must hide...

BILLINGS
You don't like the light.

DARKNESS
BURNS!

BILLINGS
All right. All right. What if…you could let me go. If you let me go, I won't tell anyone what happened. You can go hide somewhere and…

DARKNESS
Hide inside Etta.

BILLINGS
Oh. I see. Maybe I should go then.

DARKNESS
Take thing out of mouth.

BILLINGS
I…there's nothing in my mouth.

DARKNESS
ETTA MOUTH!

BILLINGS
Oh. The Jennings Gag?

DARKNESS
TAKE OUT!

BILLINGS
Yes! Ok, sorry, I…ok.

(*BILLINGS removes the brace. ETTA coughs/gags*)

ETTA
Oh thank the lord…

DARKNESS
Make Etta free.

BILLINGS
You want me to undo her restraints? I don't think that's a good…

DARKNESS
MAKE ETTA FREE!

ETTA
You're gonna want to do it, Doc. You seen what happens
when it gets mad.

DARKNESS
FREE NOW!

BILLINGS
Jesus! Yes, OK.

(She unbinds ETTA)

DARKNESS
Etta...

ETTA
It's ok, honey. It's ok.

DARKNESS
They hurt Etta.

ETTA
I know. I was there. But I'm like year-old jerky. Ain't
nothin' tougher.

BILLINGS
...please...please keep it away...

DARKNESS
Light burns, Etta.

ETTA
You wanna sleep inside me, huh?

DARKNESS
Yes. Hurt.

ETTA
But you ate up first, yeah?

DARKNESS
Ate bad lady.

ETTA
Thank you for that.

DARKNESS
All for Etta.

ETTA
I know, honey. Come on home.

(A wet, slithering sound)

BILLINGS
...oh god, oh god, oh god...

ETTA
Hold up a second.

(The slithering stops)

ETTA
Go ahead 'n break her arms and legs, ok?

BILLINGS
No!

ETTA
So she don't hurt me no more.

BILLINGS
No! Stay away!

DARKNESS
All for Etta.

(More slithering. BILLINGS screams as the DARKNESS breaks her bones. Her cries turn to defeated wimpers)

ETTA
That's real good. Now come rest.

DARKNESS
Tired. Hurt.

ETTA
I won't let no one hurt you. We look out for each other,
yeah?

DARKNESS
Etta friend. Home.

ETTA
Amen to that.

DARKNESS
Hooooome...

(A strange sucking noise as the DARKNESS flows into ETTA)

ETTA
Whew. That thing's been a part of me since I was ten.
Still feels all weird when it crawls up in me.

BILLINGS
What...what...?

ETTA
I done told you I had the Darkness in me. So did my
mama, and my grandmama...hell, been there as long as
my family been around. Probably a long time before
that too.

BILLINGS
...please...don't hurt me...

ETTA
That's just it. I never wanted to hurt nobody. I'm a nice
lady. But the Darkness gotta eat. That's what it does.

BILLINGS
Etta...

ETTA
I was real glad when the police caught me. Figured if I ended up in solitary or somethin', wouldn't no one get hurt. But life's a real kick in the pants, in'it?

BILLINGS
Don't let it eat me. Please.

ETTA
It already et. Big one like her'll keep it full for a while. But the thing is... Why you gotta hurt me? I done nothin' to you.

BILLINGS
You don't understand...

ETTA
I'm sorry 'bout your niece. Truly. But weren't me. When the Darkness needs to eat, ain't nothin' I can do.

BILLINGS
I'm sorry. I'm so sorry.

ETTA
Ah, you say that, but that's just 'cause you're scared. You ain't sorry. You think I'm some sorta ignorant redneck who likes eatin' on folk.

(The sound of a drill revving)

BILLINGS
Put that down.

ETTA
Ain't you doctors got that hippopotamus oath? Don't harm or something. When you took this drill to me... that hurt my feelin's. And my mouth, but also my feelin's.

I had no beef with you. But now...shit, I don't know.

BILLINGS
I'll do anything. Please.

ETTA
I should just walk out of here. The Darkness is all riled up, probably kill anyone what tried to stop me. But dammit, you done pissed me off good.

BILLINGS
No.

ETTA
Figure I gotta do somethin' about that, yeah?

BILLINGS
No!

ETTA
Folks always remember the "eye for an eye" part. Howzabout a little "tooth for a tooth," huh?

BILLINGS
NO!

(BILLINGS *screams as* ETTA *begins to drill into her*)

END OF PLAY

ABOUT THE PLAYWRIGHT

Joseph Zettelmaier is a Michigan-based playwright and four-time nominee for the Steinberg/American Theatre Critics Association Award for best new play, first in 2006 for ALL CHILDISH THINGS, then in 2007 for LANGUAGE LESSONS, in 2010 for IT CAME FROM MARS and in 2012 for ALL CHILDISH THINGS. Other plays include SALVAGE, THE GRAVEDIGGER - A FRANKENSTEIN PLAY, NORTHERN AGGRESSION, DR. SEWARD'S DRACULA, INVASIVE SPECIES, THE SCULLERY MAID, NIGHT BLOOMING, and EBENEZER.

POINT OF ORIGIN won Best Locally Created Script 2002 from the Ann Arbor News, and THE STILLNESS BETWEEN BREATHS also won Best New Play 2005 from the Oakland Press. THE STILLNESS BETWEEN BREATHS and IT CAME FROM MARS were selected to appear in the National New Play Network's Festival of New Plays. He also co-authored Flyover, USA: Voices From Men of the Midwest at the Williamston Theatre (Winner of the 2009 Thespie Award for Best New Script). He also adapted CHRISTMAS CAROL'D for the Performance Network.

IT CAME FROM MARS was a recipient of 2009's Edgerton Foundation New American Play Award, and won Best New Script 2010 from the Lansing State Journal. His play ALL CHILDISH THINGS won the Edgerton Foundation New American Play Award in 2011.

Joseph is a founding member of the Roustabout Theatre Company and an Associate Artist at First Folio Shakespeare, an Artistic Ambassador to the National New Play Network, and an adjunct lecturer at Eastern Michigan University, where he teaches Dramatic Composition.

MORE FROM SORDELET INK

PLAYSCRIPTS

ACTION MOVIE—THE PLAY BY JOE FOUST AND RICHARD RAGSDALE

ALL CHILDISH THINGS BY JOSEPH ZETTELMAIER

CAPTAIN BLOOD ADAPTED BY DAVID RICE

THE COUNT OF MONTE CRISTO ADAPTED BY CHRISTOPHER M WALSH

DEAD MAN'S SHOES BY JOSEPH ZETTELMAIER

THE DECADE DANCE BY JOSEPH ZETTELMAIER

EBENEZER: A CHRISTMAS PLAY BY JOSEPH ZETTELMAIER

EVE OF IDES—A PLAY BY DAVID BLIXT

FRANKENSTEIN ADAPTED BY ROBERT KAUZLARIC

THE GRAVEDIGGER: A FRANKENSTEIN PLAY BY JOSEPH ZETTELMAIER

HATFIELD & MCCOY BY SHAWN PFAUTSCH

HAUNTED BY JOSEPH ZETTELMAIER

HER MAJESTY'S WILL ADAPTED BY ROBERT KAUZLARIC

IT CAME FROM MARS BY JOSEPH ZETTELMAIER

THE LEAGUE OF AWESOME BY CORRBETTE PASKO AND SARA SEVIGNY

THE MOONSTONE ADAPTED BY ROBERT KAUZLARIC

NORTHERN AGGRESSION BY JOSEPH ZETTELMAIER

ONCE A PONZI TIME BY JOE FOUST

THE RENAISSANCE MAN BY JOSEPH ZETTELMAIER

THE SCULLERY MAID BY JOSEPH ZETTELMAIER

ANTON CHEKHOV'S THE SEAGULL ADAPTED BY JANICE L BLIXT

SEASON ON THE LINE BY SHAWN PFAUTSCH

STAGE FRIGHT: A HORROR ANTHOLOGY BY JOSEPH ZETTELMAIER

A TALE OF TWO CITIES ADAPTED BY CHRISTOPHER M WALSH

WILLIAMSTON ANTHOLOGY: VOLUME 1

WILLIAMSTON ANTHOLOGY: VOLUME 2

WWW.SORDELETINK.COM

SORDELET INK NOVELS BY DAVID BLIXT

NELLIE BLY
WHAT GIRLS ARE GOOD FOR
CHARITY GIRL
CLEVER GIRL

THE STAR-CROSS'D SERIES
THE MASTER OF VERONA
VOICE OF THE FALCONER
FORTUNE'S FOOL
THE PRINCE'S DOOM
VARNISH'D FACES: STAR-CROSS'D SHORT STORIES

WILL & KIT
HER MAJESTY'S WILL

THE COLOSSUS SERIES
COLOSSUS: STONE & STEEL
COLOSSUS: THE FOUR EMPERORS

EVE OF IDES—A PLAY

NON-FICTION
SHAKESPEARE'S SECRETS: ROMEO & JULIET
TOMORROW, AND TOMORROW: ESSAYS ON MACBETH
FIGHTING WORDS

THE MYSTERY OF CENTRAL PARK

A rejected marriage proposal and the corpse of a dead beauty confound Dick Treadwell's hopes for happiness, until his beloved Penelope sets him a task: she will marry him if he solves— *the Mystery of Central Park!*

EVA, THE ADVENTURESS

Nellie Bly's ripped-from-the-headlines novel of a poor girl determined to revenge herself upon the world, only to find that, in the battle between love and revenge, only one can triumph.

NEW YORK BY NIGHT

Setting out to solve the bold diamond robbery, millionaire detective Lionel Dangerfield finds himself in competition with Ruby Sharpe, daring young reporter for the *New York Planet*. Will "The Danger" solve the case before Ruby can steal the story—and his heart?

ALTA LYNN, M.D.

A prank goes awry and Alta Lynn finds herself wed against her will. Leaving love behind, she throws herself into the study of medicine, only to find that love has other plans for her!

WAYNE'S FAITHFUL SWEETHEART

Beautiful Dorette Lover is rescued from poverty when she finds work as an artist's model. That same day she witnesses a seeming murder. To protect the man accused, she agrees to become his bride—only to fall desperately in love with him!

LITTLE LUCKIE

Luckie Thurlow longs to be accepted by society and gain the man she loves. But she harbors a dark secret—she is the daughter of the murderous Gypsy Queen, who plans to use Luckie to gain her own revenge!

IN LOVE WITH A STRANGER

Kit Clarendon is in love! Trouble is, she doesn't know her love's name. But she is determined to track him down and force him to love her! A wild pursuit filled with disguises, desperate deeds, and declarations of love as Kit determines to go through fire and water to win him!

THE LOVE OF THREE GIRLS

An heiress in disguise, a factory girl with dreams of wealth, and a sweet child of charity are forced into rivalry when they all fall in love with the same man! Murder, fever, fallen women, and a desperate villain conspire against— *the love of three girls!*

INTO THE MADHOUSE

Never before collected! "Who is this insane girl?" asked other papers, completely taken in by Nellie Bly's plan to infiltrate Blackwell's Island. The complete reporting surrounding her daring expose, including details not included in her initial accounts and her scathing rebuttal of the doctors' excuses!

NELLIE BLY'S WORLD—Vol. 1
1887-1888

Bly's complete reporting, collected for the very first time! Starting with the stunt that made hers a household name, Nellie Bly spends her first year at the New York World going undercover to expose frauds, sharpsters and boodlers, interviewing Belva Lockwood and Hangman Joe, and tackling Phelps the Lobbyist!

NELLIE BLY'S WORLD—Vol. 2
1889-1890

Bly's complete reporting, collected for the very first time! Nellie buys a baby, has herself followed by a detective and arrested, interviews Helen Keller, champion boxer John Sullivan, and convicted would-be killer Eva Hamilton, all before setting out on her greatest stunt of all, a race around the world!

COMING SOON:
NELLIE BLY'S WORLD, Vol. 3 & 4
NELLIE BLY'S DISPATCHES, Vol. 1 & 2
NELLIE BLY's JOURNALS, Vol. 1 & 2

ALL FROM SORDELET INK